W9-BWH-695

Carlos & Carmen

Tío Time

by Kirsten McDonald
illustrated by Erika Meza

Calico Kid

An Imprint of Magic Wagon
abdopublishing.com

For Megan who found Carlos and Carmen, Heidi who helped them be their best, and Erika who brought them to life —KKM

For all of the ladies above - Megan, Heidi, and Kirsten, for dreaming them up - but also to Candice, who made sure I gave my last ounce of colour and my best lines!
—EM

abdopublishing.com

Written by Kirsten McDonald
Illustrated by Erika Meza
Edited by Heidi M.D. Elston
Designed by Candice Keimig

Library of Congress Cataloging-in-Publication Data

Names: McDonald, Kirsten, author. | Meza, Erika, illustrator.
Title: Tío time / by Kirsten McDonald ; illustrated by Erika Meza.
Description: Minneapolis, MN : Magic Wagon, [2017] | Series: Carlos & Carmen
  | Summary: It is the first snow of the season, and Tío Alex comes over to play with the twins, and cook them a special secret surprise.
Identifiers: LCCN 2015045658 | ISBN 9781624021435 (print)| ISBN 9781680779585 (ebook)
Subjects: LCSH: Hispanic American families--Juvenile fiction. | Uncles--Juvenile fiction. | Twins--Juvenile fiction. | Brothers and sisters--Juvenile fiction. | Snow--Juvenile fiction. | CYAC: Hispanic Americans--Fiction. | Uncles--Fiction. | Family life--Fiction. | Twins--Fiction. | Brothers and sisters--Fiction. | Snow--Fiction.
Classification: LCC PZ7.1.M4344 Ti 2016 | DDC 813.6--dc23
LC record available at http://lccn.loc.gov/2015045658

Table of Contents

Chapter 1
Hooray Day

Spooky patted Carlos's nose, but he did not wake up. She batted Carlos's ear, but he did not wake up.

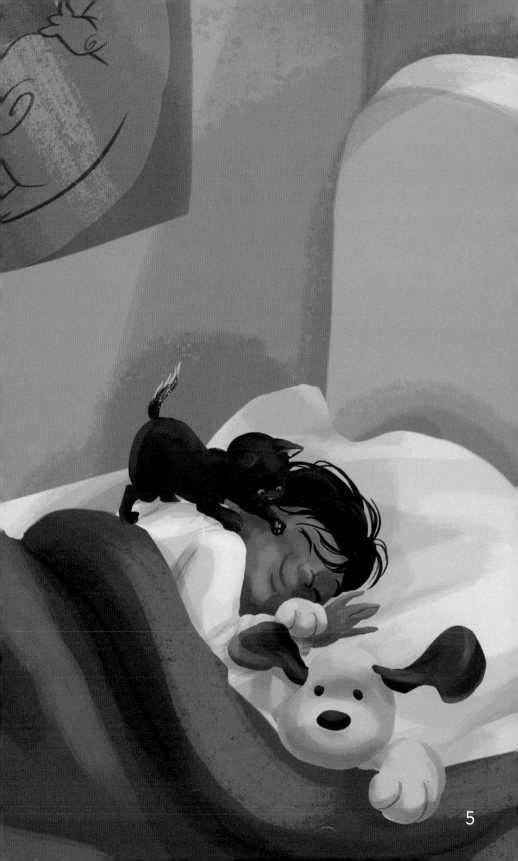

Finally, she licked his cheek with her tiny, pink tongue.

Carlos sat up in bed. "Buenos días to you too," he said.

Carlos scratched Spooky under her chin. "Your fur is cold."

Carlos rubbed her back. "Your fur is wet."

Spooky's tail slipped through his fingers. "And, ice is stuck to your tail."

Carlos jumped out of bed and looked out his window. Everything everywhere was covered in snow.

Carlos and Spooky ran into Carmen's room. They pounced on her bed.

"Get up!" Carlos shouted.

Murr-uhhh, added Spooky.

Carlos ran to Carmen's window.
"Come see what's in our yard!" he said.

"Is it Tío Alex and his secret recipe?"
Carmen asked with a yawn.

Carlos had forgotten all about Tío
Alex and his secret recipe.

"Oh boy! This is going to be a best
ever, triple-iple, hooray day! Tío Alex, a
secret recipe, and snow!" said Carlos.

"Snow!" Carmen exclaimed. She raced to the window.

Carlos and Carmen stared out at their backyard. There was snow on the bushes. There was snow on the trees. There was even snow on top of the tire swing.

"Let's go play in the snow," said Carmen.

The twins ran out of the room,
but Spooky did not. She did not like
snow. She liked warm, snugly beds.
So, she curled up in Carmen's covers
and went to sleep.

Chapter 2
Snowballs and Cocoa

Carlos and Carmen were building a snow cat in the front yard. Just then, Tío Alex drove up.

"Hooray!" shouted Carlos and Carmen. "It's Tío time!"

Tío Alex leaped out of his car and threw a snowball toward the twins. It skidded through the snow and showered them with snowflakes.

"Are you thinking what I'm thinking?" Carlos and Carmen said. And, because they were twins, they were.

"We're going to get you, Tío Alex!"

The twins hid behind the snow cat. They threw snowballs at Tío Alex, but he batted them away.

"Bet you can't catch me!" called Tío Alex.

Carlos and Carmen chased Tío Alex around and around the snow cat. They were still chasing him when Mamá called, "Hot cocoa time!"

Tío Alex scooped up the twins.

"¡Vámonos!" said Tío Alex. "The snow will wait, but your Mamá's hot cocoa will not. I hope she used her special recipe."

"Is her special recipe the same as your secret recipe?" Carmen asked.

"Nope," said Tío Alex as he stomped up the steps.

"What does your secret recipe make?" Carlos asked as they took off their boots and mittens.

"It's a secret sorpresa," said Tío Alex.

"Please tell us," begged the twins.

"It won't be a surprise if he tells you," said Mamá. She handed them each a cup of hot cocoa.

Tío Alex took a sip. "Mmm, just the way I like it, with a hint of chili powder."

"Mmm," said Carmen, "just the way I like it, with a dash of cinnamon."

"And triple-mmm," said Carlos. "Just the way I like it. With a hint of chili powder, a dash of cinnamon, and lots and lots of mini marshmallows."

19

Chapter 3
The Secret Recipe

When all the hot cocoa was gone, Tío Alex and the twins went back outside. They rolled giant snowballs and built a snow fort.

They made snow angels, and they
played snow soccer. Then they shook
the smallest trees and snow tumbled
down all over them.

Tío Alex wiped the snow from his
face. "Is anyone hungry for the secret
Mexican recipe?" he asked.

"Me!" Carlos shouted.

"¡Yo también!" Carmen agreed.

"Tell us what it is," said Carlos.

"Nope," said Tío Alex as they walked into the house. "But, I'll give you some clues. It has queso and chorizo and is one of my favoritos."

Carmen guessed nachos. Carlos guessed tacos. Then they both guessed burritos.

Finally, Tío Alex said, "I'm keeping it secret. So stop guessing and start cooking!"

Tío Alex gave Carlos the white cheese to grate. He gave Carmen the orange cheese to grate.

When all of the cheese was grated, Tío Alex held up a big bag. He said, "And, now for my secret ingredients. No peeking, you two."

Carlos and Carmen heard plastic peeling, and they heard a big pan rattling.

Finally, Tío Alex said, "No looking in the oven while we wait."

And just to be sure, he hung a towel over the window in the oven door.

Chapter 4
The Yummy Surprise

Mamá and Papá came into the kitchen just as the timer beeped. "Yum," said Carmen, sneaking toward the oven.

"Yummy-yum!" agreed Carlos, reaching for the towel.

Tío Alex shooed them away from the oven. "Sit down, and I will get the sorpresa. No peeking," he told them.

Carlos and Carmen covered their eyes. Spooky brushed against their legs under the table. She was hoping for a taste of the yummy surprise.

Tío Alex banged the oven door shut and said, "Let's eat."

The twins uncovered their eyes. They could not believe what they saw. "Pizza!"

"But, you said the recipe was from Mexico," said Carmen.

"And, you said it was something our abuela makes," added Carlos.

"It is!" Tío Alex said with a laugh. "This is your grandmother's sausage and cheese pizza."

"It's one of my favorites," said Mamá.

Carmen blew on her pizza slice and took a bite. "Thiff if the beft piffa," she said.

Tío Alex gave Spooky a small piece of cheese.

"Wow!" Carlos said as he finished his first bite. "Our abuela knows how to make the best pizza in Mexico!"

Carmen shook her head from side to side. "No, Carlos, our abuela knows how to make the best pizza in the world!"

Then everyone made plans for more snowy fun as they ate the best pizza ever.

Spanish to English

abuela – grandmother

buenos días – good morning

chorizo – sausage

favoritos – favorites

Mamá – Mommy

Papá – Daddy

queso – cheese

sorpresa – surprise

Tío – Uncle

¡Vámonos! – Let's go!

¡Yo también! – Me too!